This edition published by Kids Can Press in 2020

Originally published in Japan by Bronze Publishing Inc., Tokyo, under the title
Boku no Tabi © 2018 Akiko Miyakoshi

Text and illustrations © 2018 Akiko Miyakoshi
English translation by Cathy Hirano
English translation © 2020 Kids Can Press

Kids Can Press gratefully acknowledges the financial support of the
Government of Ontario, through the Ontario Media Development Corporation.

Published in Canada and the U.S. by Kids Can Press Ltd.
25 Dockside Drive, Toronto, ON M5A 0B5

Kids Can Press is a Corus Entertainment Inc. company

www.kidscanpress.com

English edition edited by Yvette Ghione

Printed and bound in Malaysia in 10/2019 by Tien Wah Press (Pte) Ltd.

CM 20 0 9 8 7 6 5 4 3 2 1

Library and Archives Canada Cataloguing in Publication

Title: I dream of a journey / [written and illustrated by] Akiko Miyakoshi.
Other titles: Boku no tabi. English
Names: Miyakoshi, Akiko, 1982– author, illustrator. | Hirano, Cathy, translator.
Description: Translation of: Boku no tabi. | Translated by Cathy Hirano.
Identifiers: Canadiana 20190176717 | ISBN 9781525304781 (hardcover)
Classification: LCC PZ7.M682 Ia 2020 | DDC j895.63/6 — dc23

I Dream of a Journey

Akiko Miyakoshi

Kids Can Press

This is my hotel. Small but cozy,
it's my pride and joy.

I can't remember how long ago
I welcomed my very first guests.

Lots of people from all over
the world come to stay.

They tell me stories of
places I've never seen.
And I tell them
stories of my little town,
because I know all there
is to know, you see.

Late at night, my workday done,
I crawl into bed.
As I close my eyes to sleep, I feel
a great yearning to go far, far away.

In my dreams, I set off on a journey.
With a big suitcase.

I get on a plane and travel from one new
place to another.

I roam freely, wherever I want.

On the way, I stop to visit old friends, guests
who've stayed at my hotel over the years.
Maybe their friends will welcome me, too.

When I'm traveling, each day
brings unexpected happenings.
I collect these special moments,
treasuring them in my heart.

I wonder …
As I travel farther and farther away,
will I begin to miss my own little hotel?

Morning comes.
I'm still here.

Time to start another day.
New guests will be arriving soon.

In the evening, my workday done, I sit in my worn old chair and read over letters from my friends. Their notes from all over the world make me want to travel, too.

Maybe one day I'll be standing in the same places shown on their postcards.

I look at each one closely.

I've never been anywhere but this little town.
And yet …

One day, I just might set off on a journey.

I'll take a big suitcase,
leave this town,
leave this country …

I bet everyone will be surprised.

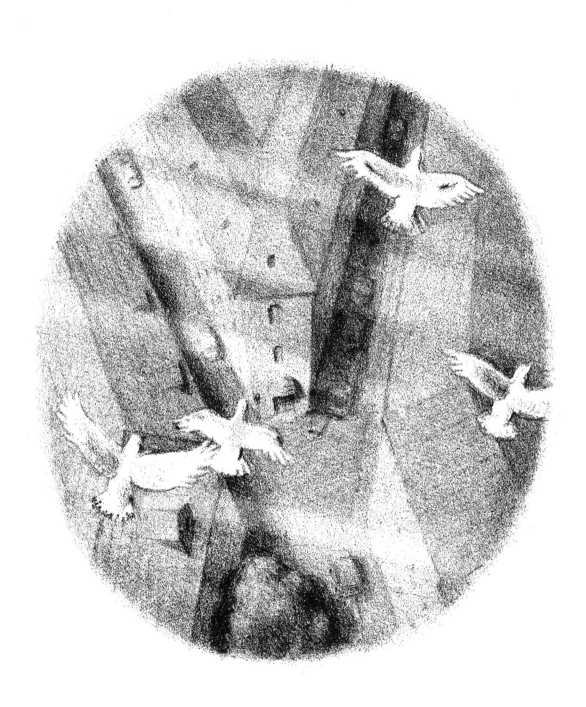